Bear on a B[ike]
Ours à vélo

Stella Blackstone
Debbie Harter

Barefoot Books
Step inside a story

**Bear on a bike,
As happy as can be,
Where are you going, Bear?
Please wait for me!**

Ours à vélo,
Heureux comme un roi,
Où vas-tu, Ours ?
S'il te plait, attends-moi !

I'm going to the market,
Where fruit and flowers are sold,
Where people buy fresh oranges
And pots of marigold.

Je vais au marché,
Où l'on vend des fleurs et des fruits,
Où l'on achète des oranges parfumées
Et des pots de soucis.

Bear on a raft,
As happy as can be,
Where are you going, Bear?
Please wait for me!

Ours en radeau,
Heureux comme un roi,
Où vas-tu, Ours ?
S'il te plait, attends-moi !

I'm going to the forest,
Where fearsome creatures prowl,
Where raccoons play and bobcats snarl
And hungry foxes howl.

Je vais dans la forêt,
Où rôdent de redoutables créatures,
Où s'amusent les ratons laveurs et grondent les lynx
Et où renards affamés n'hésitent pas à japper.

Bear on a wagon,
As happy as can be,
Where are you going, Bear?
Please wait for me!

Ours en chariot,
Heureux comme un roi,
Où vas-tu, Ours ?
S'il te plait, attends-moi !

I'm going to the prairie,
Where wild buffaloes roam,
Where graceful eagles soar and glide
And prairie dogs make their home.

Je vais dans les vastes herbages,
Où courent les buffles sauvages,
Où planent les aigles gracieux
Et dorment la nuit les chiens de prairie.

Bear in a steam train,
As happy as can be,
Where are you going, Bear?
Please wait for me!

Ours en train à vapeur,
Heureux comme un roi,
Où vas-tu, Ours ?
S'il te plait, attends-moi !

I'm going to the seaside,
Where children love to play,
Where young friends dig and race
And swim, while fishes dart away.

Je vais à la mer,
Où les enfants aiment jouer,
Où les amis creusent, courent et nagent
Et les poissons s'échappent au large.

Bear on a boat,
As happy as can be,
Where are you going, Bear?
Please wait for me!

Ours en bateau,
Heureux comme un roi,
Où vas-tu, Ours ?
S'il te plait, attends-moi !

I'm going to an island,
Where magic star fruits grow,
Where herons fish in secret groves
And sparkling rivers flow.

Je vais sur une ile,
Où poussent des caramboles magiques,
Où les hérons vont pêcher parmi des arbres fruitiers
Et les rivières scintillantes n'ont de cesse de couler.

**Bear in a balloon,
As happy as can be,
Where are you going, Bear?
Please wait for me!**

Ours en montgolfière,
Heureux comme un roi,
Où vas-tu, Ours ?
S'il te plait, attends-moi !

I'm going to a rainbow,
Where the earth meets the sky,
Where the clouds turn into rain
And bright-winged parrots fly.

Je vais voir un arc-en-ciel,
Où la terre s'unit au ciel,
Où les nuages se changent en pluie
Et où les perroquets colorés sont nombreux à voler.

Bear in a carriage,
As happy as can be,
Where are you going, Bear?
Please wait for me!

Ours en carrosse,
Heureux comme un roi,
Où vas-tu, Ours ?
S'il te plait, attends-moi !

I'm going to a castle,
Where night is turned to day,
Where princes and princesses dance
And merry music plays.

Je vais au château,
Où la nuit devient jour,
Où la musique joyeuse fait tourner
Princes et princesses qui aiment danser.

**Bear on a rocket,
Flying through the night,
Wherever you are going, Bear,
Goodbye and goodnight!**

Ours en fusée,
Traversant la nuit,
Où que tu ailles, Ours,
Au revoir et bonne nuit !

Vocabulary / Vocabulaire

bike – le vélo

raft – le radeau

wagon – le chariot

train – le train

boat – le bateau

balloon – la montgolfière

carriage – le carrosse

rocket – la fusée

Barefoot Books
2067 Massachusetts Ave
Cambridge, MA 02140

Barefoot Books
29/30 Fitzroy Square
London, W1T 6LQ

Text copyright © 1998 by Stella Blackstone
Illustrations copyright © 1998 by Debbie Harter
The moral rights of Stella Blackstone and Debbie Harter have been asserted

First published in Great Britain by Barefoot Books, Ltd
and in the United States of America by Barefoot Books, Inc in 1998
The bilingual French edition first published in 2017
Translated by Jennifer Couëlle
Reproduction by Bright Arts, Hong Kong
Printed in China on 100% acid-free paper
This book was typeset in Futura and Slappy
The illustrations were prepared in watercolor, pen and ink, and crayon

ISBN 978-1-78285-328-2
British Cataloguing-in-Publication Data:
a catalogue record for this book is available from the British Library
Library of Congress Cataloging-in-Publication Data
is available upon request

1 3 5 7 9 8 6 4 2